Dark M

Second series

The Dark Candle	
The Dark Machin	978-184167-601-2
The Dark Words	978-184167-602-9
Dying for the Dark	978-184167-604-3
Killer in the Dark	978-184167-605-0
The Day is Dark	978-184167-606-7
The Dark River	978-184167-745-3
The Bridge of Dark Tears	978-184167-746-0
The Past is Dark	978-184167-747-7
Playing the Dark Game	978-184167-748-4
The Dark Music	978-184167-749-1
The Dark Garden	978-184167-750-7

First series

The Dark Fire of Doom	978-184167-417-9
Destiny in the Dark	978-184167-422-3
The Dark Never Hides	978-184167-419-3
The Face in the Dark Mirror	978-184167-411-7
Fear in the Dark	978-184167-412-4
Escape from the Dark	978-184167-416-2
Danger in the Dark	978-184167-415-5
The Dark Dreams of Hell	978-184167-418-6
The Dark Side of Magic	978-184167-414-8
The	-421-6
The	-413-1
The	-420-9

Dark Man

Playing the Dark Game
by Peter Lancett
illustrated by Jan Pedroietta

Published by Ransom Publishing Ltd.
Radley House, 8 St. Cross Road, Winchester, Hampshire, UK
SO23 9HX
www.ransom.co.uk

ISBN 978 184167 748 4

First published in 2011

A CIP catalogue record of this book is available from the British Library.

Dark Man

Playing
the Dark Game

by Peter Lancett

illustrated by Jan Pedroietta

Rans⚬m

Chapter One:
The Children

The Dark Man is in a shopping precinct. He is talking to the Old Man.

'A little girl and a little boy are in danger,' the Old Man says.

'Where are they?' the Dark Man asks.

'They are trapped in the ruined big house, way outside the city.'

The Dark Man nods.

He knows where this house is.

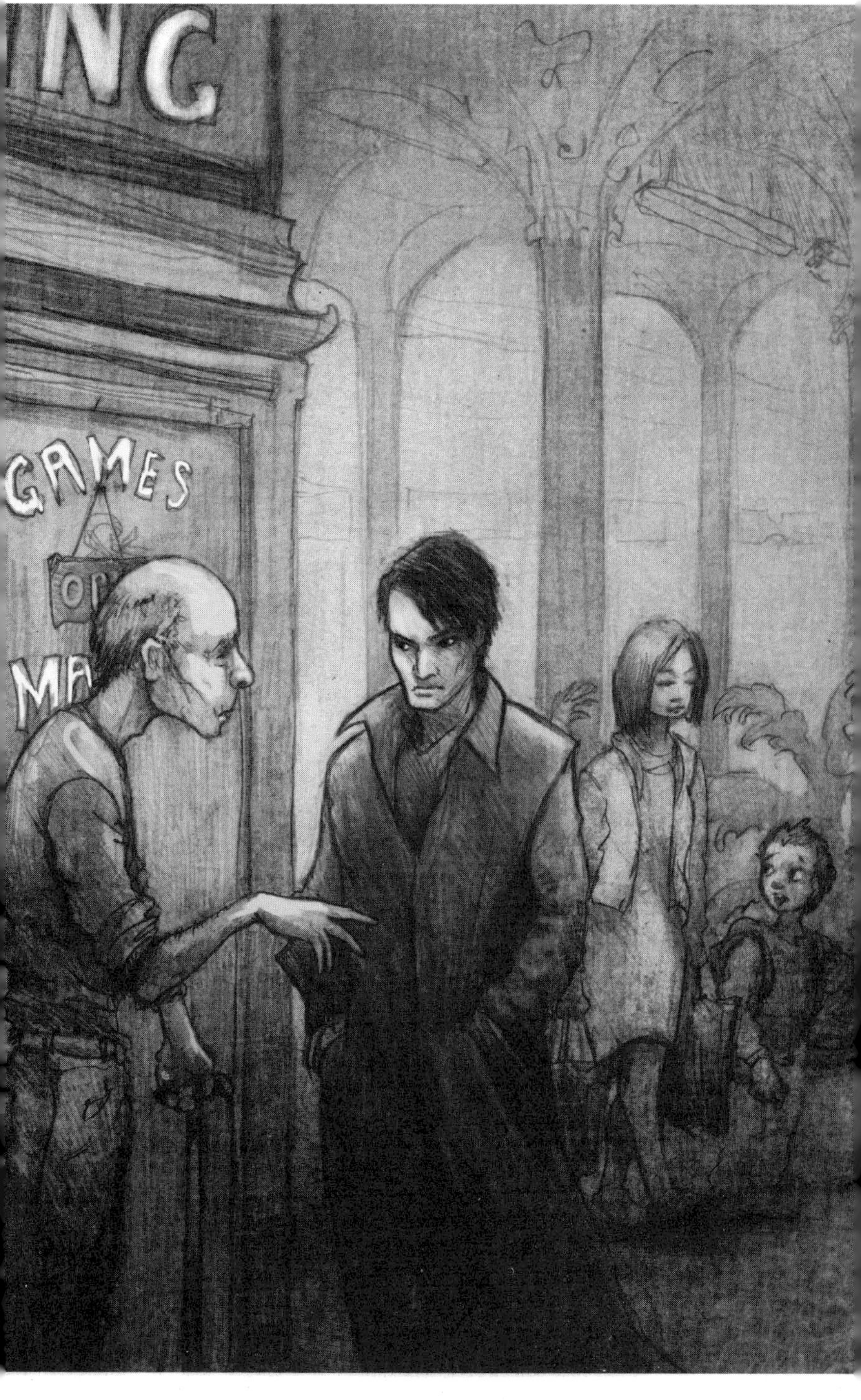
NG
GAMES

'Magic protects the house during daylight,' the Old Man continues. 'You can only enter after dark.'

'Why are these children special?' the Dark Man asks.

'Because together, they can see magic charms that are invisible to you and me.'

'I will set them free tonight and bring them to you,' the Dark Man says.

The Old Man watches the Dark Man walk away.

Then he notices a small shop.

He is drawn to the window.

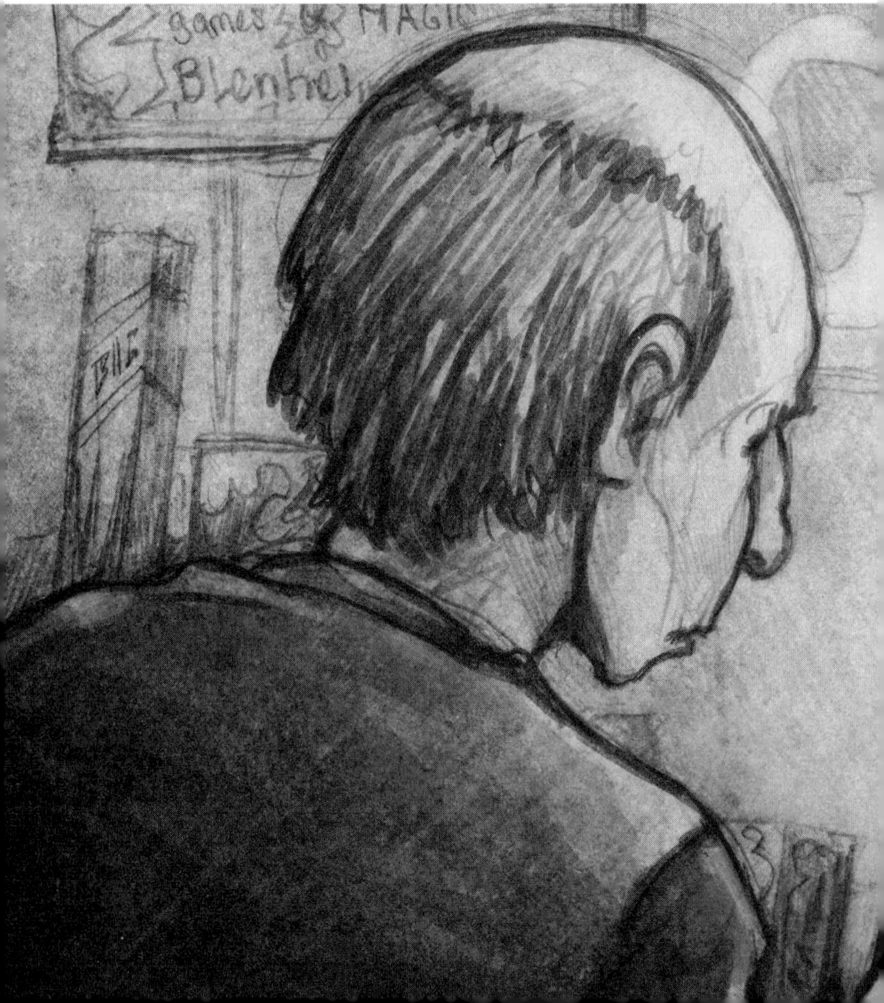
games

In the window, he sees a box with a picture of a dark, ruined house on the lid. It is a game.

This must be a sign, he thinks, as he goes into the shop to buy this strange game.

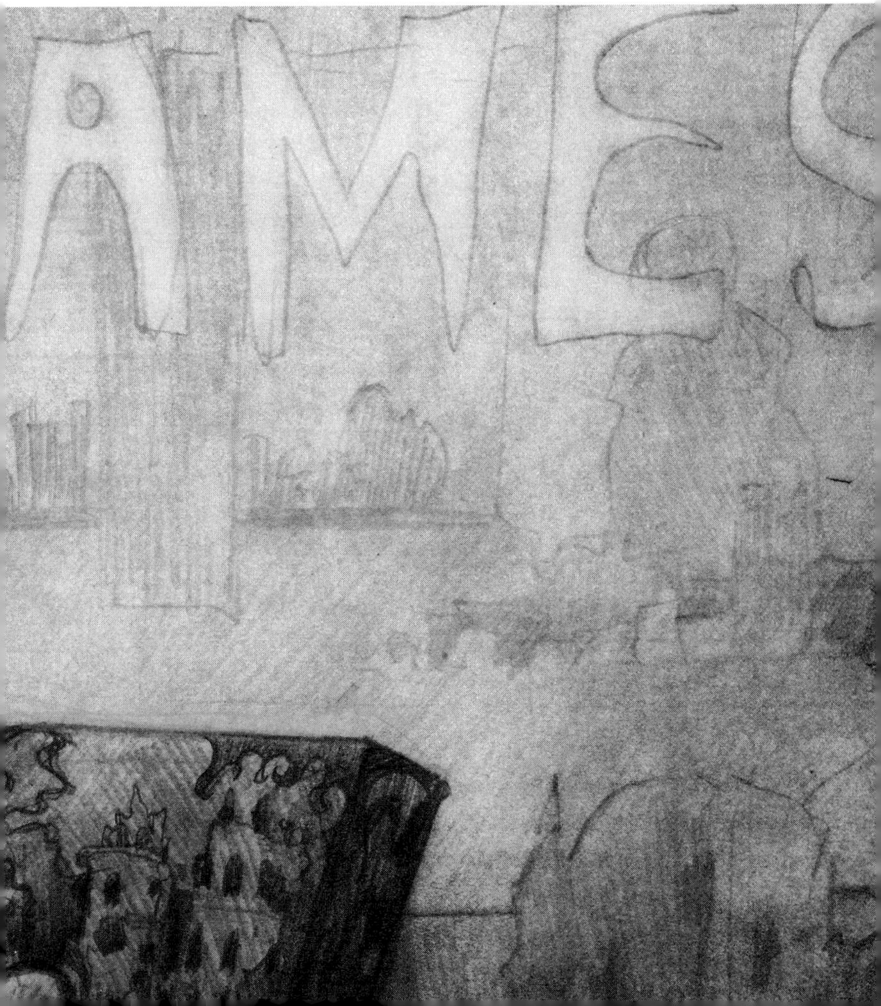

At night, the Dark Man stands before the massive doors of the ruined house.

He reaches out to push one of them.

The Old Man was right.

The house can be entered after dark.

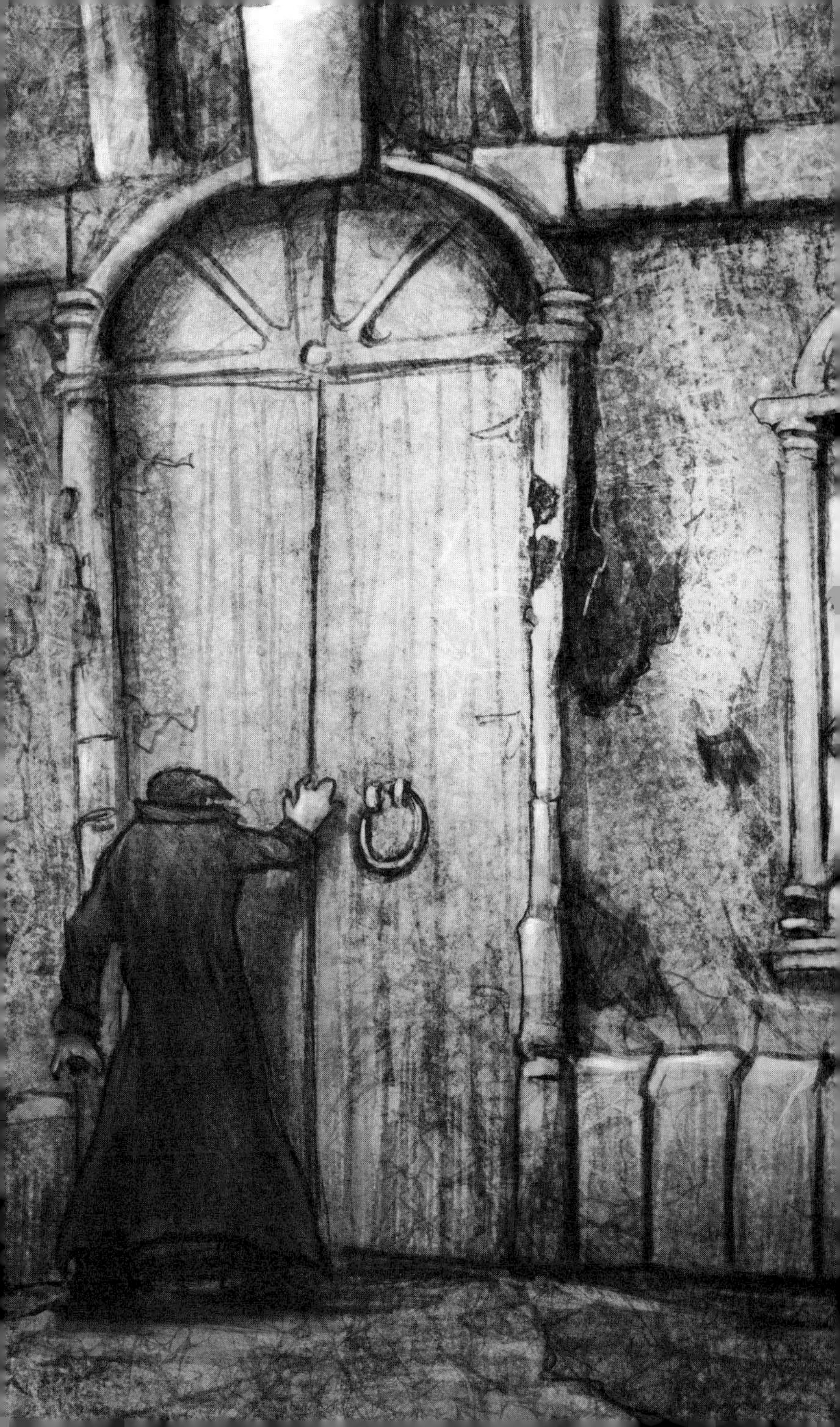

The heavy door swings open slowly.

The Dark Man steps inside.

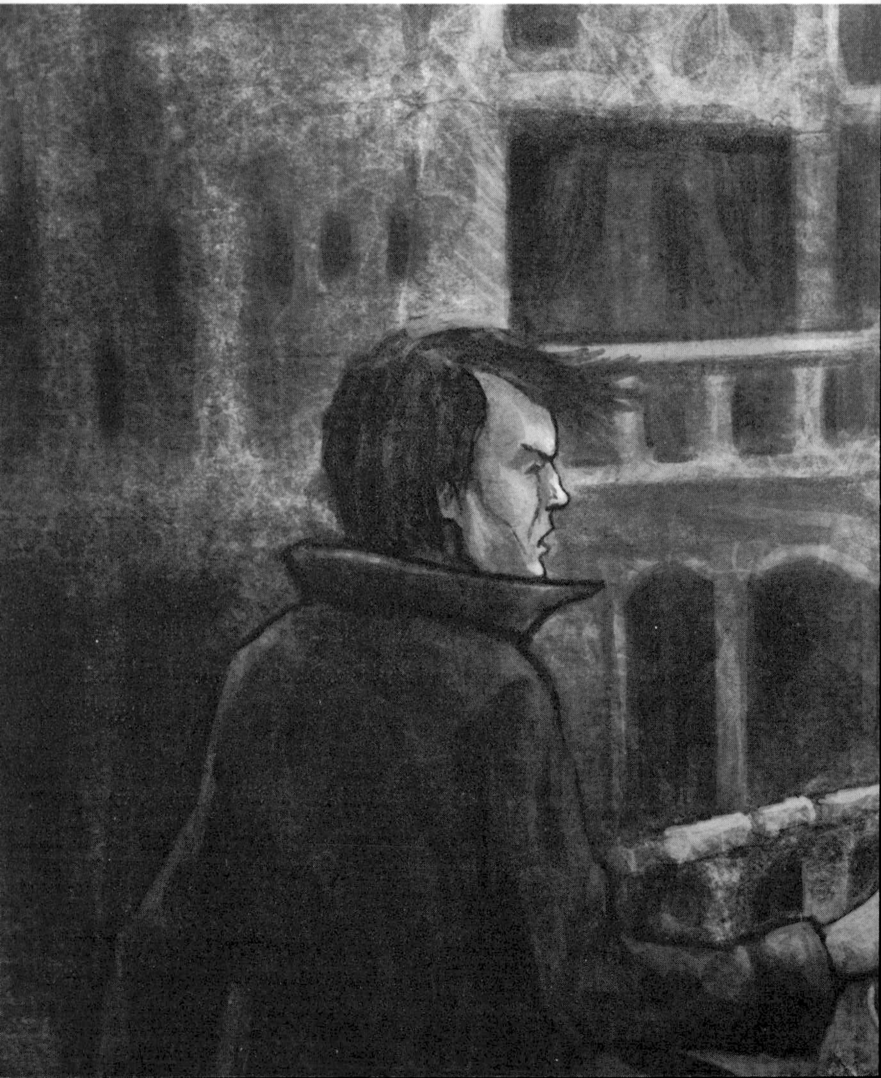

He walks carefully towards a grand staircase.

At the bottom of the stairs, he stops.

He can hear the sound of children sobbing. It is coming from upstairs.

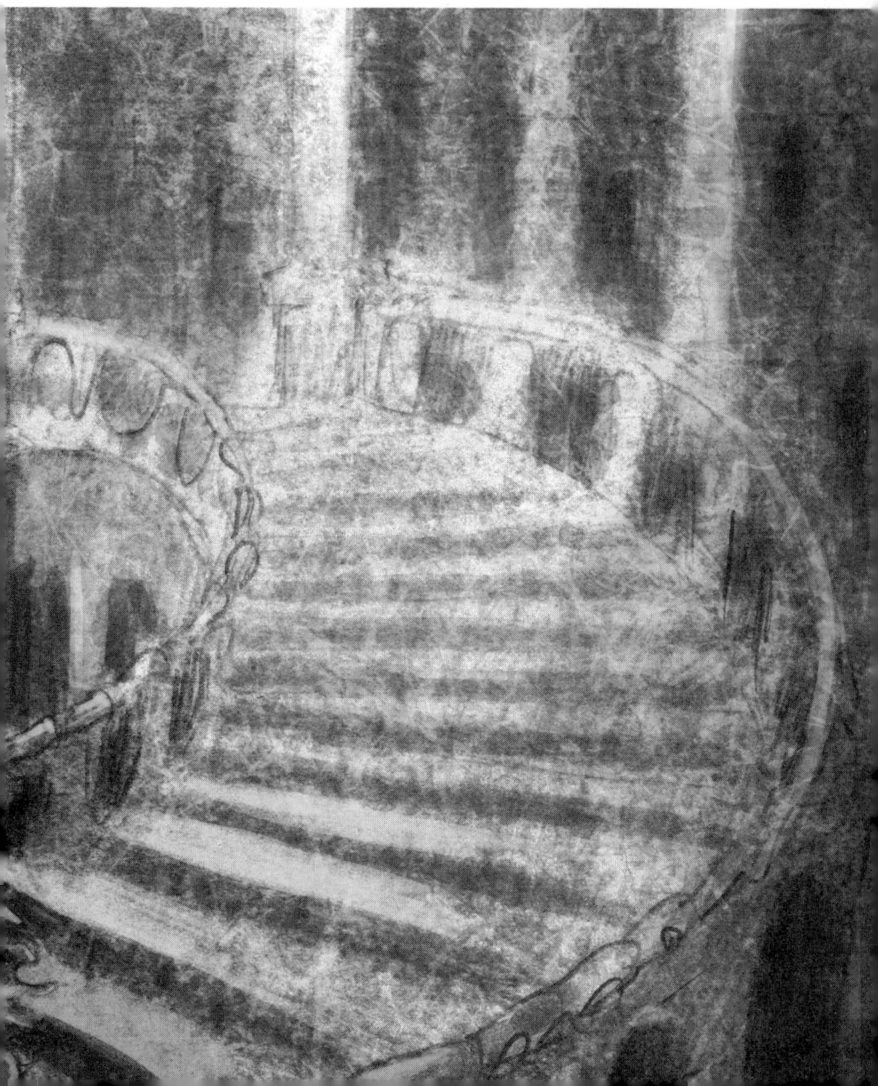

Chapter Two:
The Game

In a room lit by glass globes that store sunlight, the Old Man sits at a table.

He has the game board spread out, and on it are printed gloomy corridors and rooms.

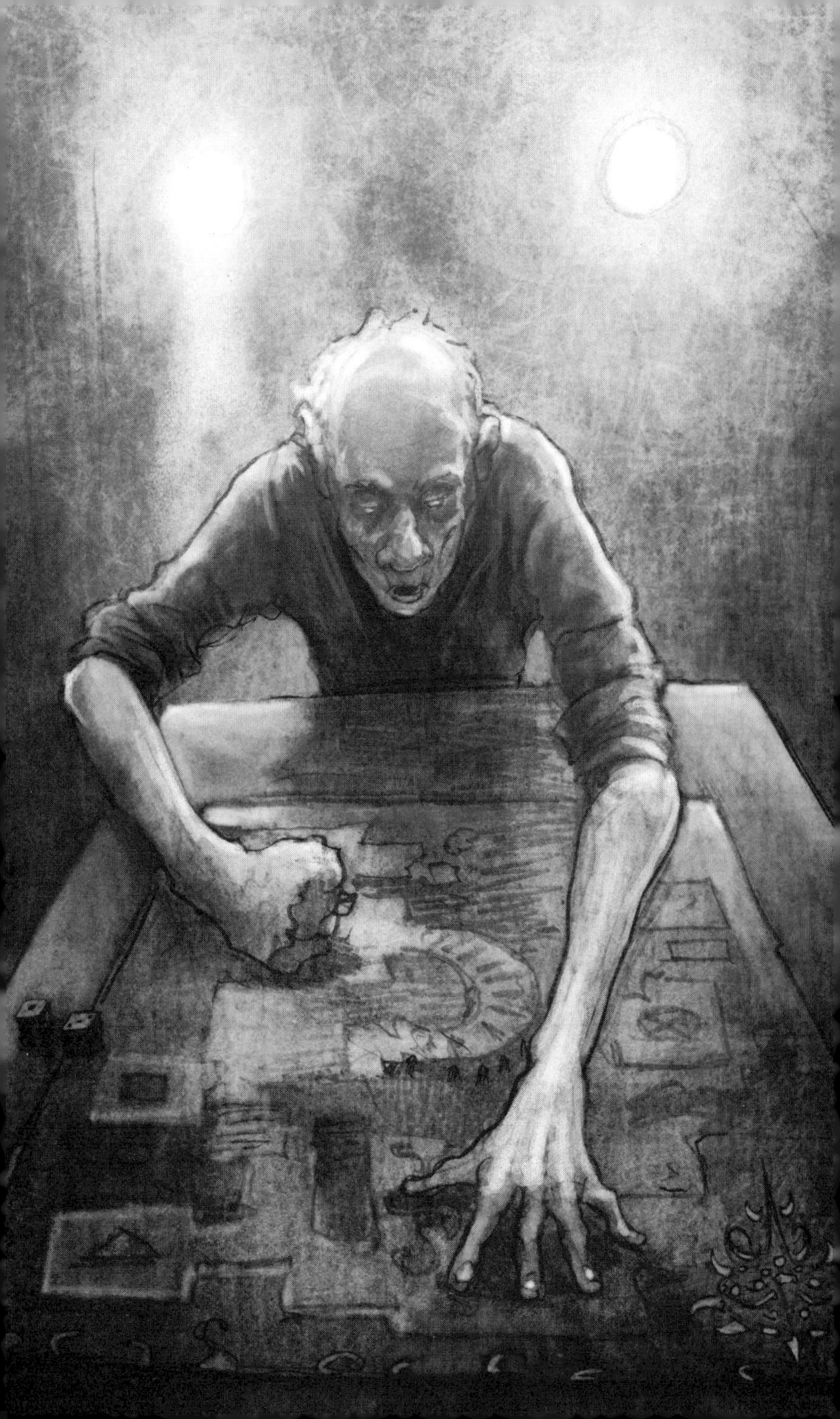

The Old Man rolls the dice.

On the board, one of the rooms lights up.

There is a large, black dog in this room.

The Old Man goes to roll the dice again, but cannot lift them off the board.

It is not his turn.

The dog could turn out to be good or bad.

Across the city, another room is gloomy, lit by candles.

A Shadow Master sits at a rough table.

He is playing the same game as the Old Man.

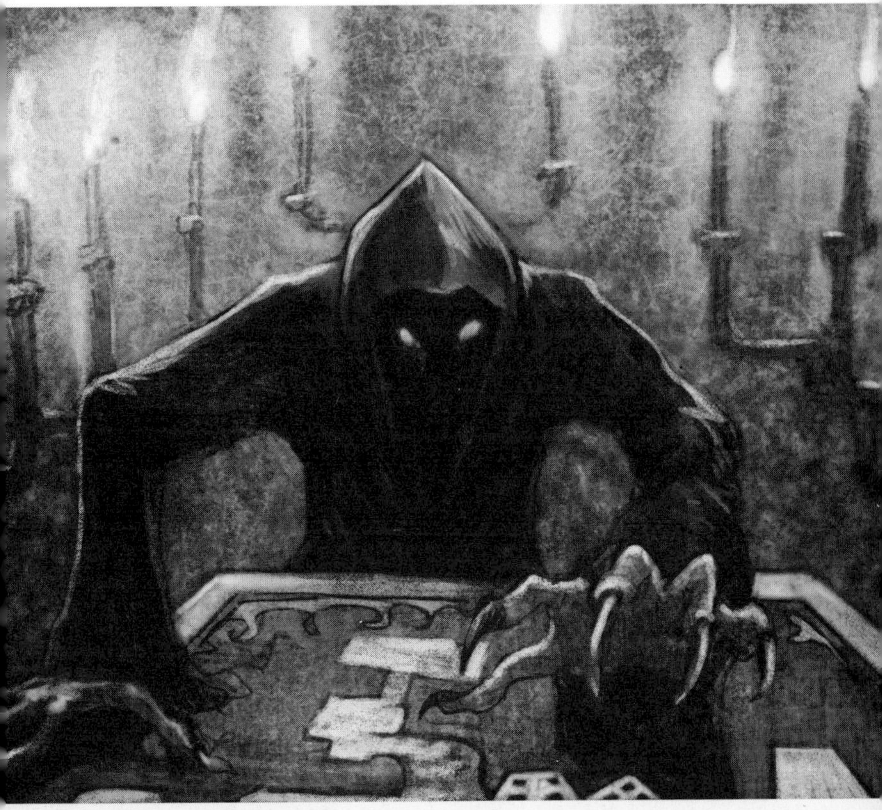

The Shadow Master picks up his own dice and lets them fall on the board.

The numbers are a one and a two.

They are not high enough to let him influence the dog.

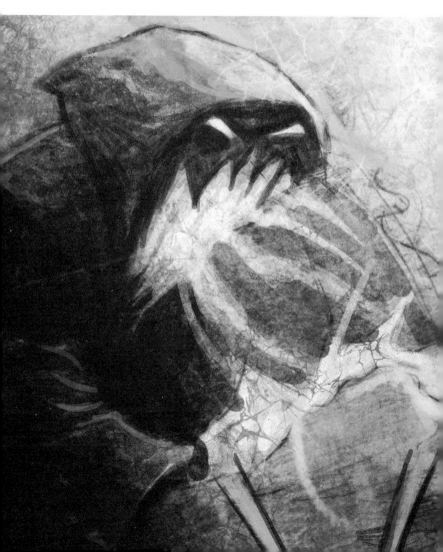

On the board, the dog seems to wag his tail.

The Shadow Master screams in rage and brings a fist down hard on the table.

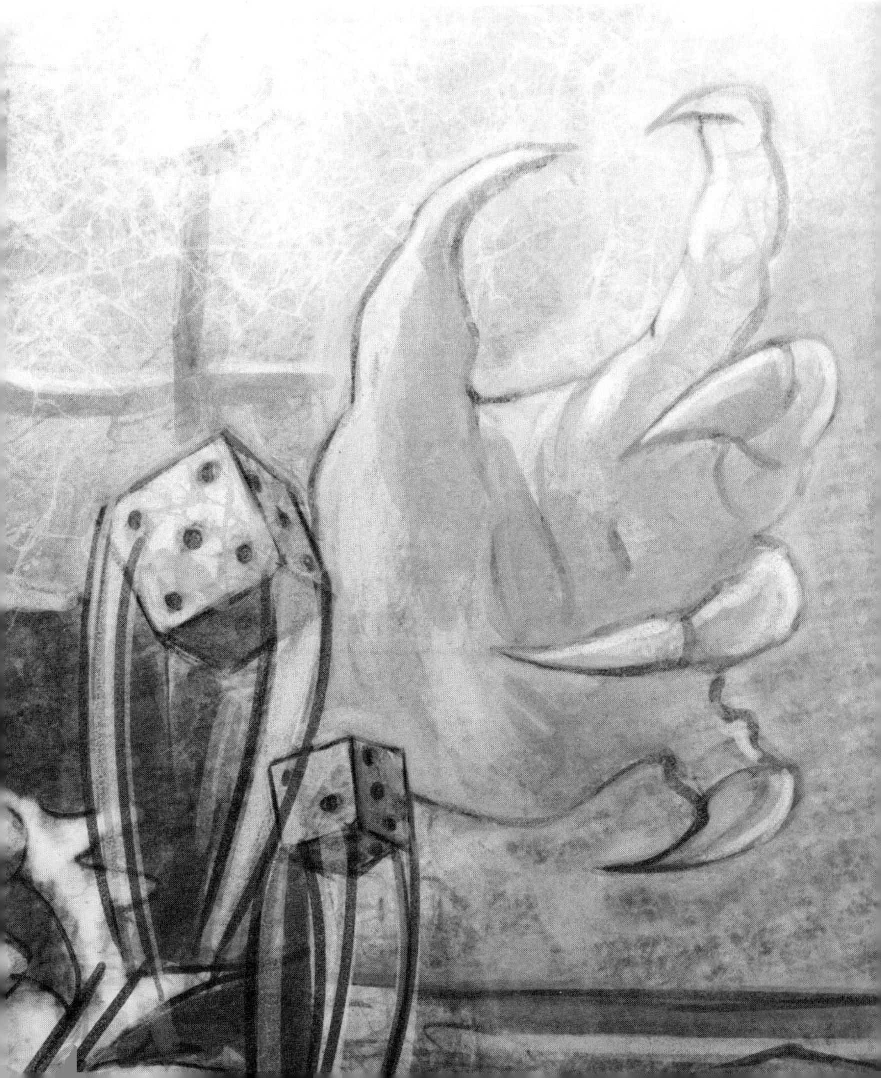

Back in the ruined house, the Dark Man is at the top of the stairs.

He sees light coming from under a door, and he hears a dog bark.

He makes his way to the lighted room and opens the door.

The black dog inside wags his tail.

The dog sniffs the Dark Man's legs, and he pats it on the head.

They both look up as they hear the sound of children crying.

The dog starts to walk along the corridor. The Dark Man follows.

They wander through the dark house, until they come to a door that is like no other.

This black door is shut very tight.

The dog barks once, and they hear sobbing.

The Dark Man pushes at the door, but it will not move.

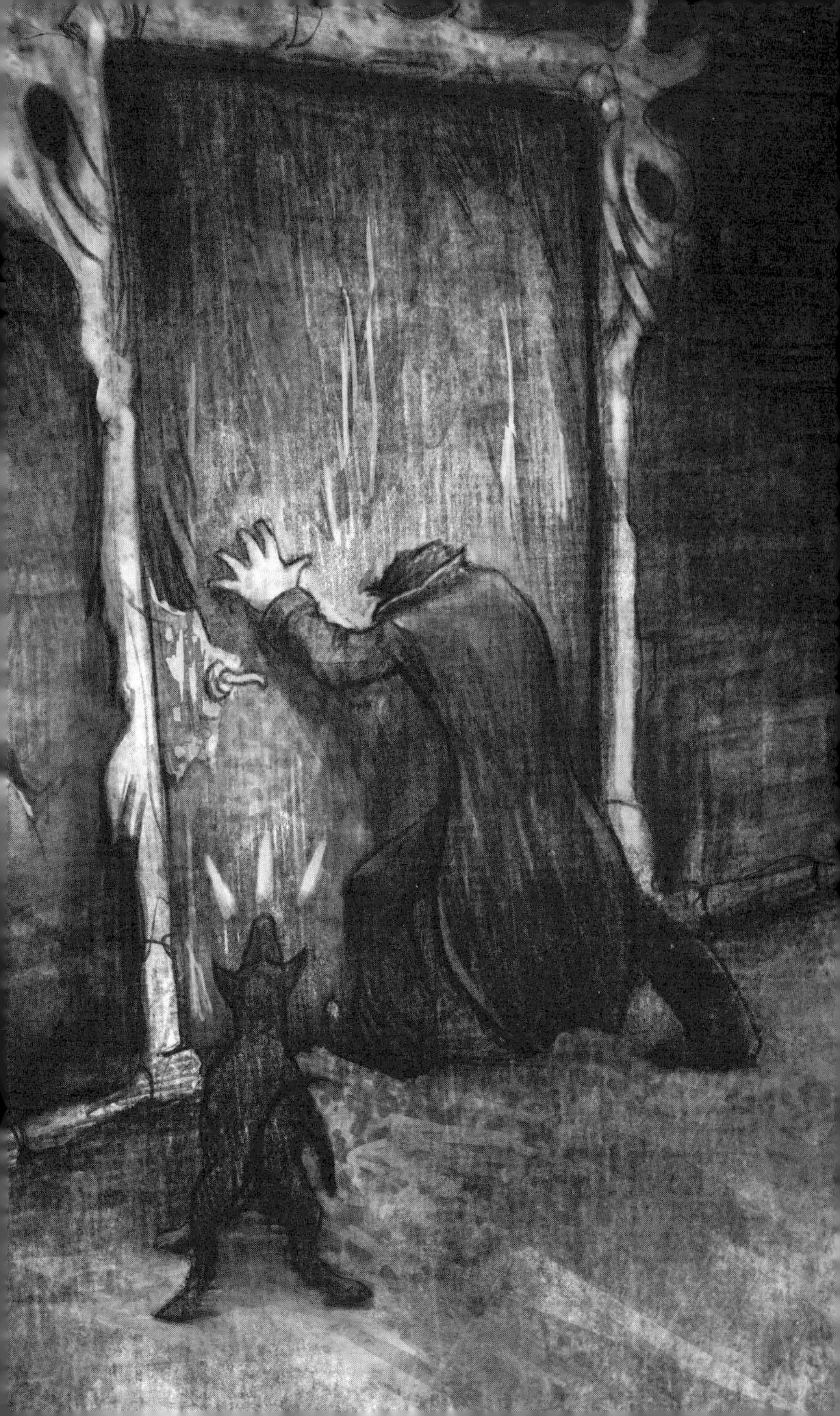

Chapter Three:
A Dog, A Man and A Snake

In his room, the Old Man notices that a room on his game board has become totally black.

He picks up his dice and lets them fall.

A six and a five.

On the board, light glows at the edges of the blackened room.

He can see a man and a dog outside the room.

He knows that the man is the Dark Man.

The Dark Man pushes at the black door and opens it.

Inside, a little boy and a little girl are holding each other tight.

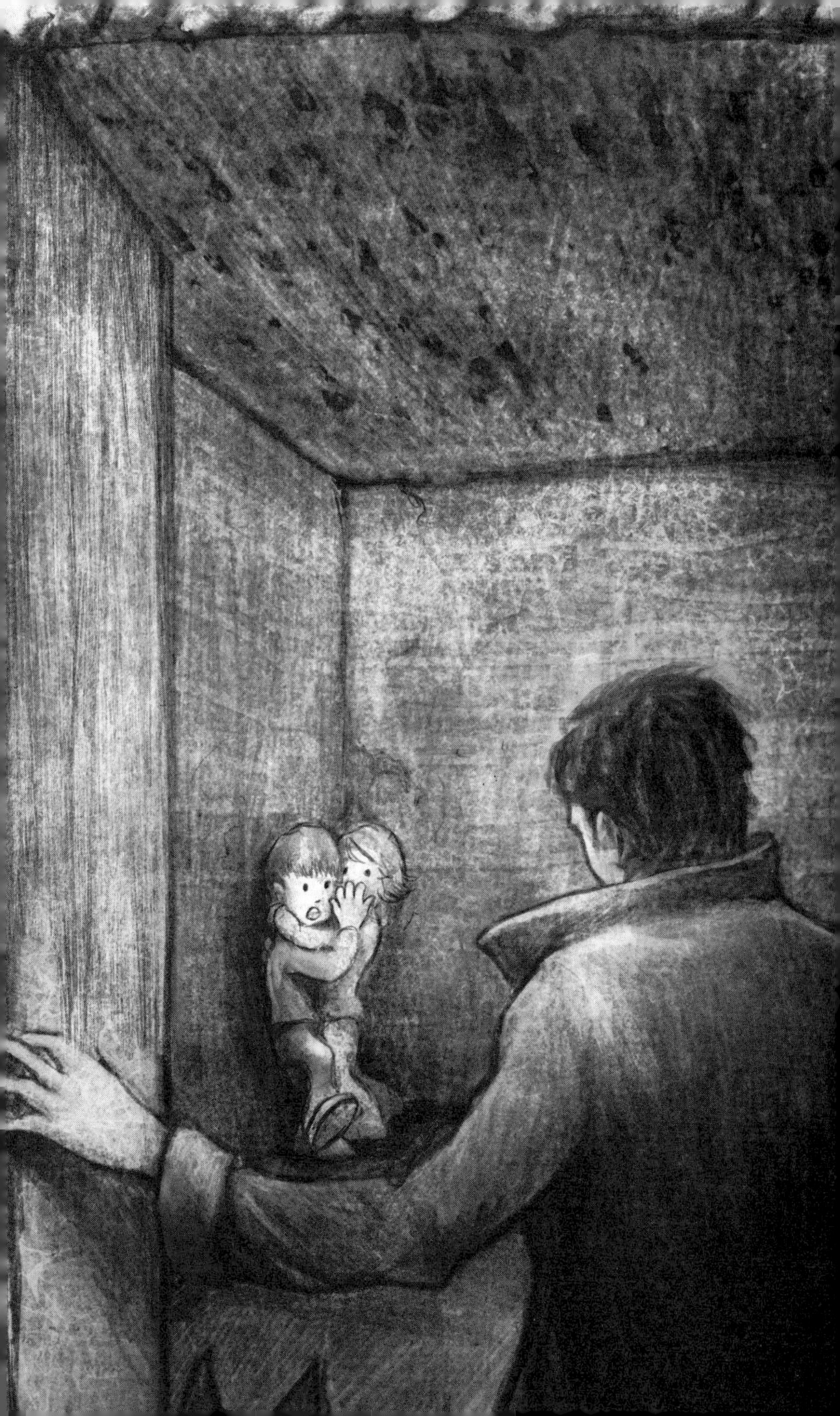

'I have come to rescue you,' the Dark Man says.

The children run across the room towards him.

But a huge snake rises from the floor and stops them.

They are afraid of the snake.

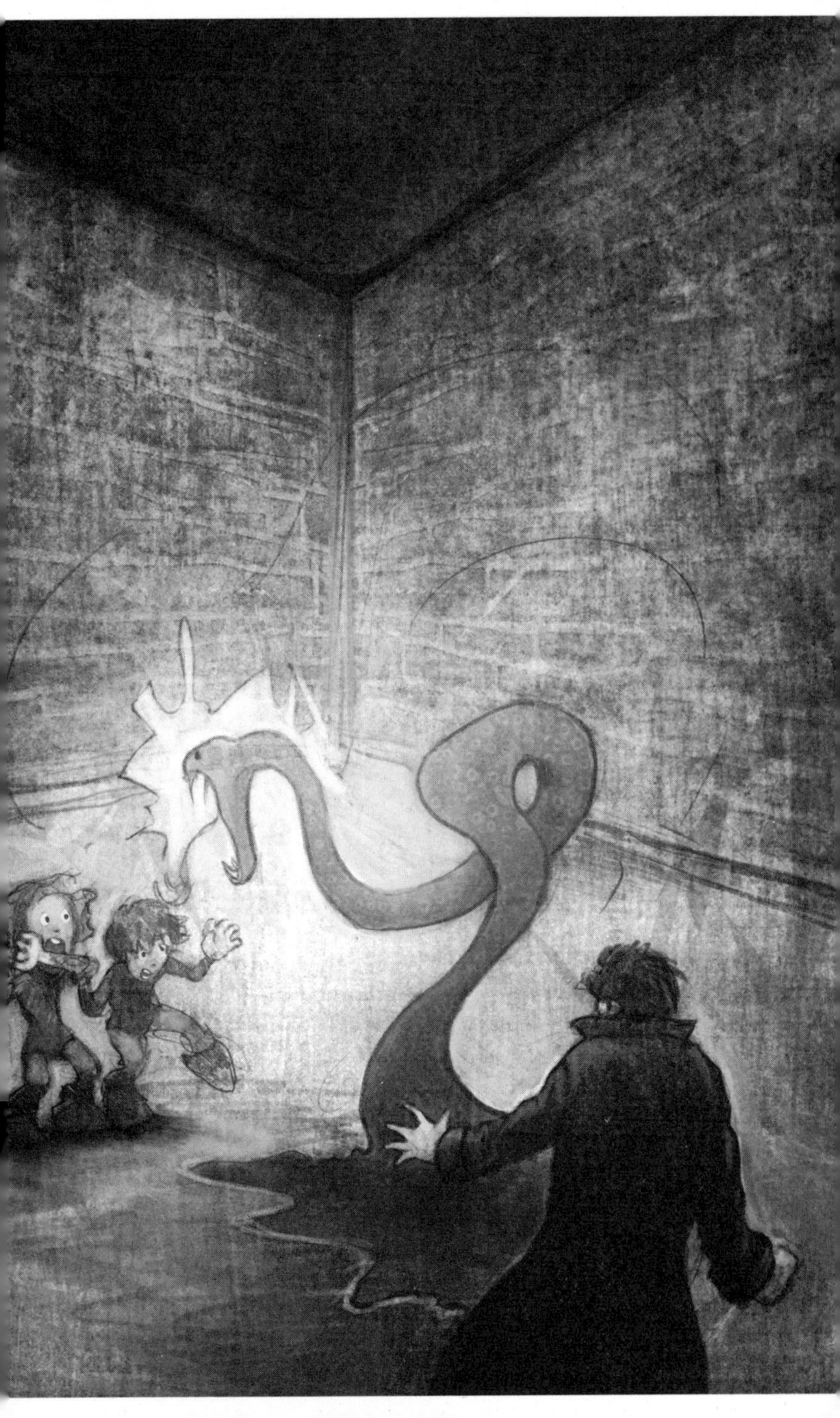

In the city, the Shadow Master laughs.

On the table, his dice show a five and a five.

He can now control the snake.

On the board, he sees it hissing at the children.

The dog leaps into the room and bites at the snake.

The snake backs off, into a far corner.

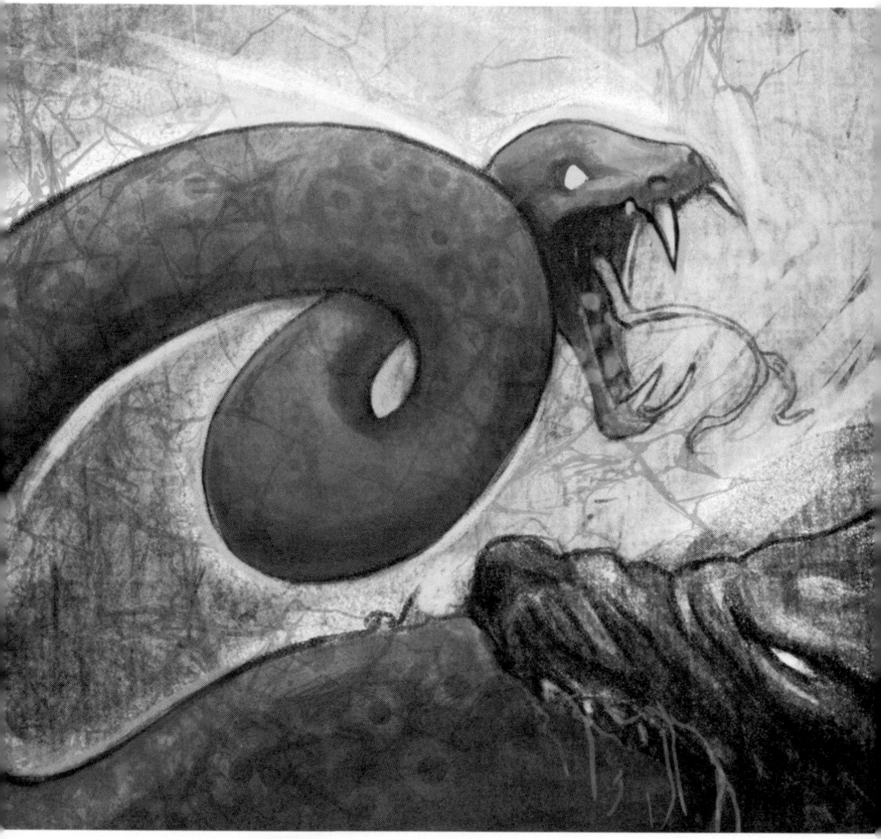

'Come on, quickly,' the Dark Man calls out to the children.

Together they run from the room.

Chapter Four:
A Good Score

The Shadow Master is in a rage.

He picks up his dice and lets them fall.

He has thrown a six and a six, the highest score possible.

It will make the snake stronger than the dog.

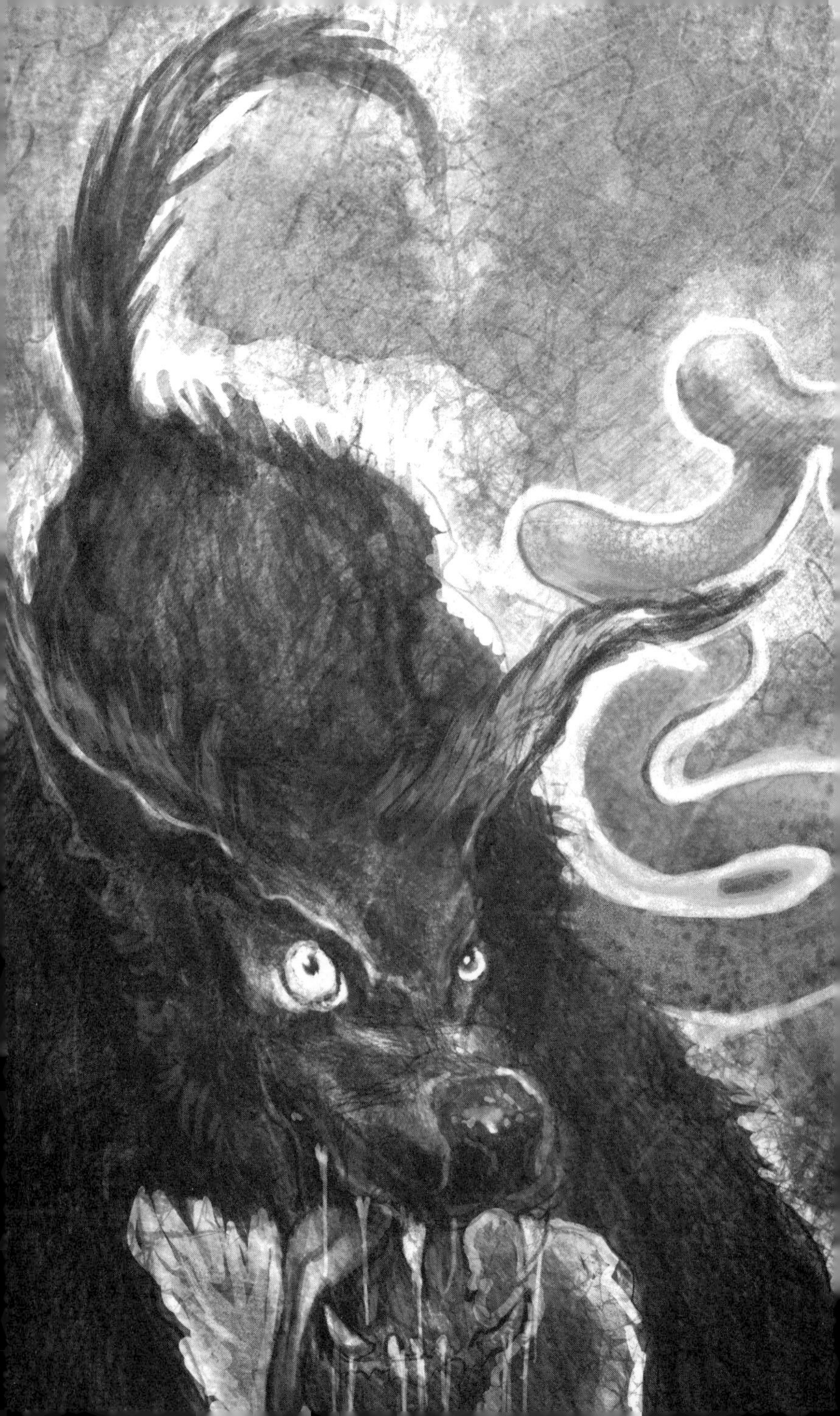

As the Dark Man and the children escape, the snake strikes quickly and bites the dog.

The dog yelps, and falls to the floor.

But then, it starts to rise.

It is getting bigger and bigger.

It is becoming a snarling monster.

The Old Man can see what is happening.

The children and the Dark Man are at the main doors.

But the doors are shut fast, and the monster dog is closing in on them.

On his board, the Old Man sees the doors glow.

He needs to throw a good score if the doors are to open.

He lets the dice tumble.

A five and a four.

The Dark Man pushes at the door.

He has to use all of his strength, but he does manage to push it open.

The children rush outside and he follows them.

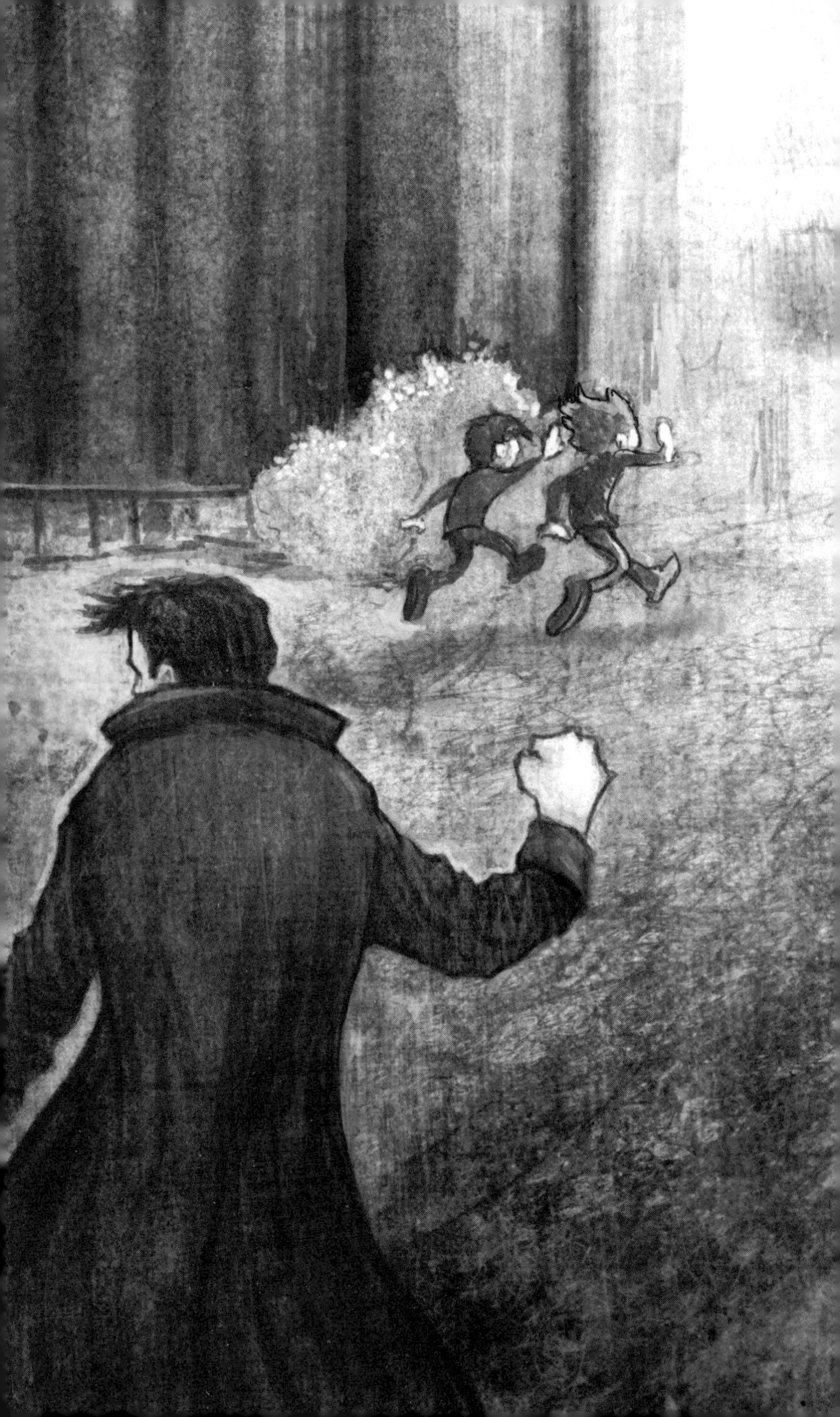

He slams the door shut, moments before the monster dog can reach them.

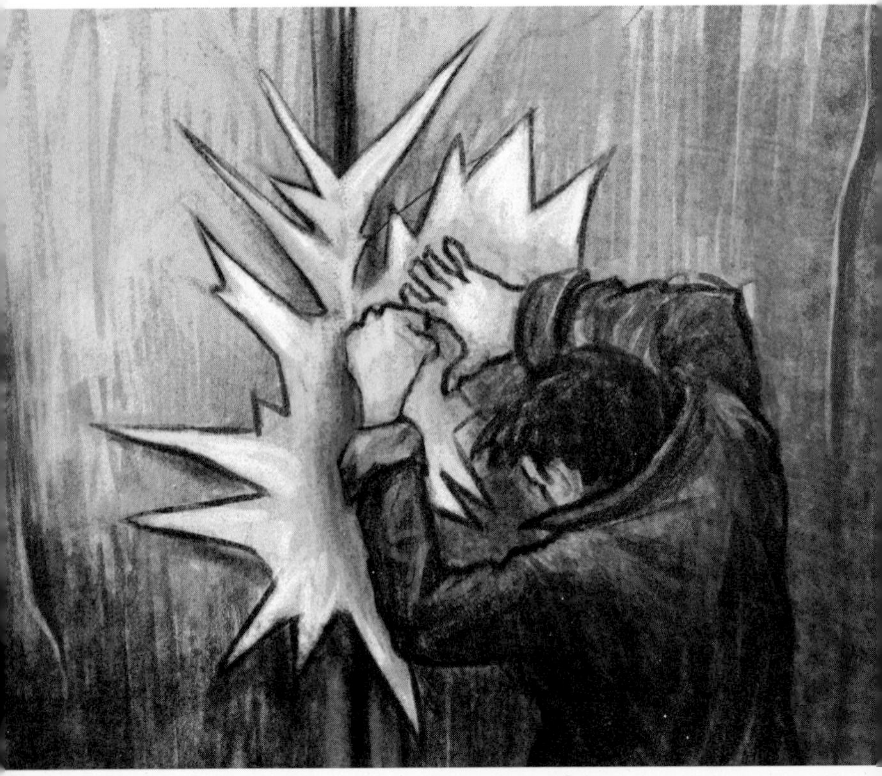

They hear the dog howling and scratching at the door, but they are safe.

It has been a close call.

'I'm Ben,' and 'I'm Joanne,' the children say, holding his hands.

'We're very glad that you are good at games.'

The Dark Man shakes his head.

'I wasn't playing,' he says.

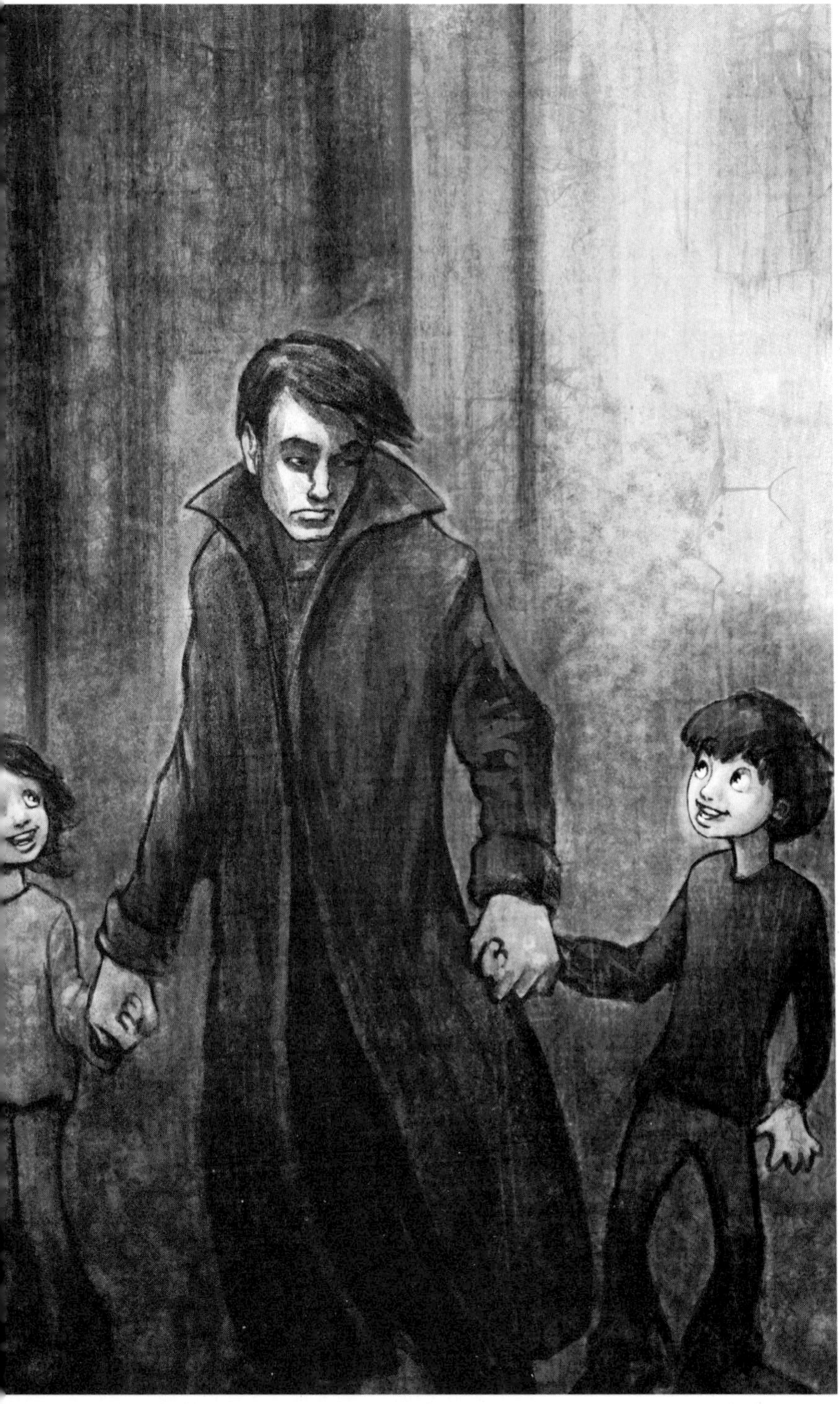

But he wonders what the children mean.

He will have to ask the Old Man.

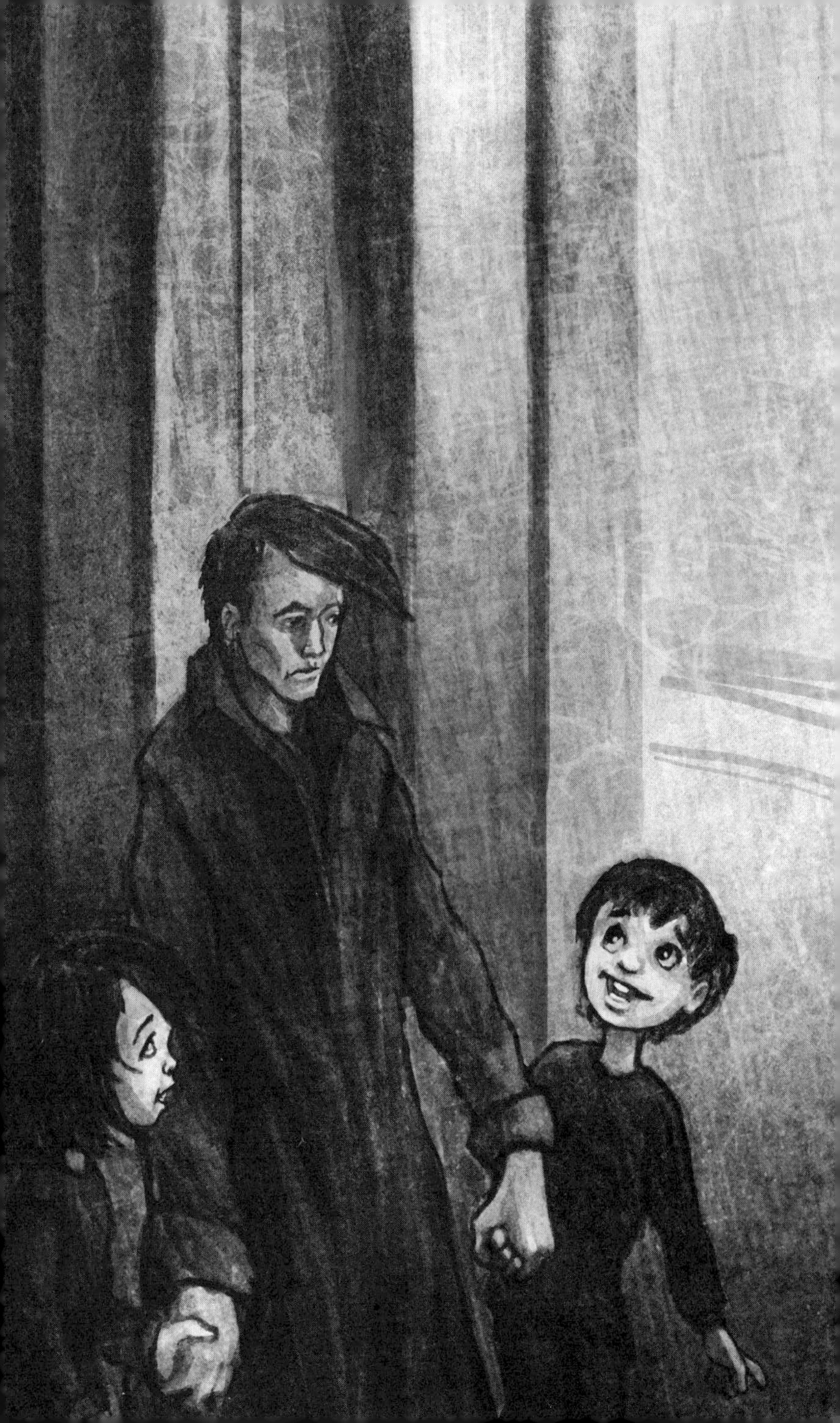

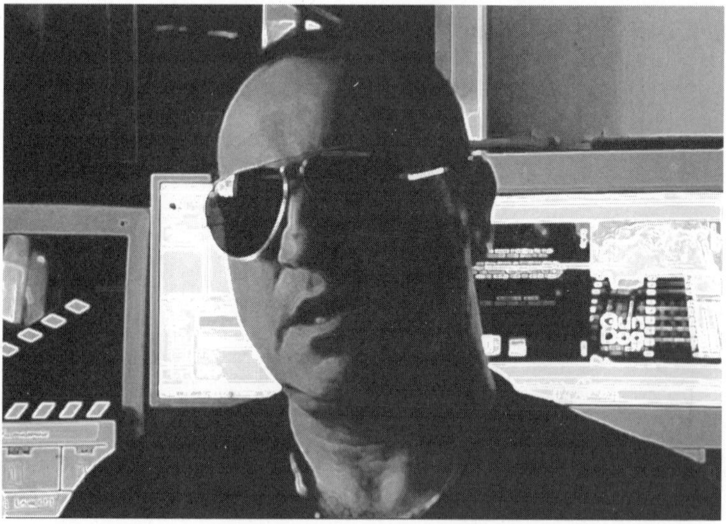
Gun
Dog

The author

Peter Lancett is a writer, editor and film maker. He has written many books, and has just made a feature film, *The Xlitherman*.

Peter now lives in New Zealand and California.